Cho
Your
Own Death

Written by Marianna Shek
and
Illustrated by Tara Brown

Rock on kitty

First published 2015 by Rock On Kitty Publications
www.rockonkitty.com.au

ISBN: 978-0-9942666-0-6

To our families - James Warr, Leanne Brown and Tony Brown (otherwise known as 'mum and dad, my two favourite hobbits').

1

They found another dead kid yesterday. Sally Ellerson. You weren't good friends but you remember going to her birthday party. She wore a cheeky grin and a milk moustache as everyone chimed 'Happy Birthday'. When the police announced they found her body in the cooling vat of the chocolate factory, all you could see was the toothless smile ghosted upon her face. There are only five kids left in Goultown. It's time to do something.

'I'll be next I bet.' Angus Chorley hunches further into the library chair but he still towers head and shoulders over everyone. You refrain from rolling your eyes. Angus is easily the biggest seventh grader at Goultown Primary so God knows what he's freaking out about. 'I stood next to her at the party. The murderer's systematically killing everyone from her party.'

'I stood on her other side and I'm still alive,' you correct nervously.

This doesn't boost morale. Probably because everyone's remembering the kid standing behind Sally – Noel the Nose-picker. Suffocated in class when he shoved two fingers up his nostrils and got stuck. The coroner found cookie crumbs and hundreds and thousands glued together by a giant booger that probably caused the blockage. A few days later, Leah Reiner died after ballet class because her bun was too tight. She hadn't even been invited to Sally's birthday party. Both freak accidents – or were they?

'I think there's a connection,' you say slowly, 'but it's not Sally's birthday party. Maybe we should just leave it to the police.'

'The grown-ups are in on this, including the police and your parents,' Jessica declares. She's got a fervent glow in her eyes as she looks up from her pile of library books. She's one of those kids who think the answers are always in a book. Come to think of it, in her chequered skirt and turtleneck, she bears a striking resemblance to Nancy Drew. 'Haven't you noticed how every time a kid dies, it's the grown-ups who find the body? And they're always feeding us lame excuses for why we can't leave town.'

Angus' little sister Tammy pipes up indignantly, 'That's not true! Mum and Dad were all for taking us out of town until it's safe but they couldn't find the car keys.'

Jessica arches an eyebrow and smiles condescend-ingly. Tammy is four years younger than everyone.

'I don't think they're in on it,' you say slowly trying to keep the peace, 'but they're just so oblivious! The grown-ups think Goultown is all white picket fences and happily-ever-afters. My dad thinks the others kids have just run away. And my mum reckons I'll be fine as long as I don't talk to strangers or loiter after school.'

'Ha! Soon there'll be no kids left to attend school,' Jessica declares. 'We need to hole up in a safe place where there are no grown-ups. Like the abandoned orphanage.'

'As if that's going to work,' scoffs one of the boys you've never liked. Frankie Dufont. He keeps slamming his right fist into his other hand like he's fielding a softball game. 'I say we track down the killer ourselves. Go straight to the chocolate factory and look for clues.'

Everyone is looking at you expectedly. You realise by calling the meeting you've become the unofficial leader of the group.

You decide to barricade inside the abandoned orphanage (Turn to page 9)

You decide to look for clues at the chocolate factory (Turn to page 4)

2

The chocolate factory is the main tourist attraction in Goultown. When your cousin visited from out of town, your parents made you take him. He thought it'd be a magical chocolate factory with chanting dwarves and syrupy waterfalls. Boy, was he disappointed.

Doctor Choc is an eccentric food scientist who runs his factory like a sterile laboratory with complicated machines named mass spectrometers and gas chromatographers. There's also the warehouse section where a multi-level conveyor belt with lots of cogs and chains goes upwards, downwards and even sideways if you crank the levers right. This is where the workers mix, pound and package Doc Choc Chocolate Bars. This is where Sally Ellerson's body was found swirling through the choc-chip, peanut butter mixture.

Jessica's mum works at the chocolate factory so it's easy for you to organise a tour. While the others watch the production line, you slip away to chat with Jessica's mum. You've known Mrs Porter all your life since you and Jessica went to kinder-garten together.

'Of course I knew the dead girl.' Her tight lips suggest not only did she know Sally but she heartily disapproved of her. She's an efficient packer. Fill box with chocolate. Close flaps. Seal with tape.

'Let me help you carry that.' You grab the box and place it on the trolley.

'Thanks Drew. You're a good kid.' She's chewing her lower lip. Fill box with chocolate. Close flaps. Seal with tape. 'Doctor Choc's good to us workers. Good to the kids too. Once a month, he collects all the cracked chocolate and sweets we can't sell and gives them away to the local school for fundrais-ing. And he used to give a lot of bars to the orphanage before orphans stopped being a thing. But that Sally girl got greedy. Even though Doctor Choc was practically handing out bars for free, she'd come nosing back to steal more chocolates. I hate working the front counter. We're accountable when stock gets lifted. She was a bratty kid. That's all I'm saying.'

You can see Jessica waving you over from across the warehouse.

'You kids gonna be here much longer? The floor will be empty soon. We're taking a coffee break.'

'Go right ahead Mrs Porter. We won't touch anything.' You put the last box onto the trolley and head over to the others. You're fighting against traffic. The workers are clamour-ing to get out for their coffee break.

'Seems like Sally was a thief. It's probably a case of Santa sorting out the naughty from the nice. We've got nothing to worry about.' You breathe a sigh of relief. Mrs Porter said so herself. You're a nice kid.

'Don't be so sure.' Jessica has pulled up her tablet. She spends more time looking at the screen than at you. 'Apparently the murderer didn't just dump her body in the cooling vat. She was drowned. Death by chocolate.'

'Bitter sweet,' Frankie sniggers. He dips a finger into the container filled with liquid chocolate and licks it.

'Stop that! You're contaminating the chocolate,' Jessica snaps.

'The Doctor told me I could. Said it's a burnt batch anyway and they're not going to use it.' Frankie deliberately lowers his hand into the chocolate molten and brings it out. He wiggles his fingers in front of Jessica. Chocolate drips onto the floor.

'How'd you know it was the Doctor?' you ask.

Frankie licks a rivulet of chocolate trickling down his arm. 'He was in a hurry but we could see the tail of his lab coat flapping behind him.'

The chocolate smells divine. If the Doctor said they weren't going to use it, why let it go to waste? You tentatively dip a finger into the chocolate fudge sauce. On your other side, Jessica dips a plastic spoon into the tub.

You roll back your sleeves to better cup the gooey goodness. As your hands submerge, something grabs your wrist.

At first you're confused. Perhaps you're caught on the machine cogs. You yank upwards. A bowl-shaped head bobs to the surface and grins at you. Its skin is pale with a green, slimy sheen to it. The others leap back in horror.

You try to unhook its webbed hands from your wrists but it's surprisingly strong. Its eyes, small, greedy slits, study you as it grins mischievously.

'It's a kappa!' Jessica screams. 'A chocolate kappa!'

CHOOSE YOUR OWN DEATH

'What the hell is that?' You start to yell but with a graceful twist of its goblin-like body, the kappa ducks underneath the surface. You're yanked off your feet and into the pool. Angus grabs your legs, pulling you back. For a moment, you're suspended like a half-dipped churro.

Angus' grip is slipping. You squeeze your eyes shut as your head submerges. Chocolate floods your ears, mouth and nostrils. There's a strange calmness in this gluggy underworld. You can hear Jessica screaming but it's a muffled, faraway sound. You open your mouth to scream. Chocolate floods in. Everything goes brown.

THE END
(Return to page 3)

3

The house is still perched at the top of the hill, although the white washed walls have faded and the window shutters have fallen off their hinges. A winding road leads from the bottom of the hill to the front door. In the past, visitors who braved the track could look up and catch a glimpse of the wispy children, barefoot and tangled hair, running through the thick thistles, caught in a secret childhood game. Now all you see is a rusty swing set – one rubber seat still swinging as if a child had jumped off only moments ago. The rope suspending the swing has almost rotted through.

Since grown-ups decided it wasn't responsible to abandon babies in baskets with a tear-splotched letter, the orphanage hasn't fared so well. Nowadays, there's always a spare key under the Welcome Home doormat and some cookies and UHT milk in the pantry. No one knows who replaces these items. And no one knows what happened to the old Matron who used to run the orphanage and disappeared last year. Some say she still scavenges in the nearby woods.

The orphans were the first to disappear. The press hadn't paid much attention because being an orphan had fallen out of fashion. You remember it was on a Sunday because your mum was annoyed. She liked to dawdle with the crosswords page over breakfast, but that particular Sunday the cryptic crossword had been taken out to make room for a small write up about the missing orphans.

You're glad you insisted on stopping at the supermarket first. Cookies, chips, frozen party pies, soft drink, more soft drink.

'Junk food,' Frankie mumbles, spraying cookie crumbs across the counter.

'It's not a party, you know.' Angus glares at him.

Frankie smirks. 'Thought that's what you told your parents. You and your sister are staying at Drew's and Drew told his parents he was staying with me, which by the way, they'll never buy. Like I'd ever invite Drew over for a sleepover. And Jessica's mum thinks she's at young leader's camp. So chill out, Big A.'

Jessica snatches the rest of the cookies and stows them away in the pantry. 'I think Angus is less worried about getting caught by our parents and more about – oh, you know, the crazy serial killer after us!'

It's time for diversionary tactics. You send Jessica and Angus to check out the rest of the house while you, Frankie and Tammy put away the food.

'So who do you think is doing this?' Tammy asks.

'Who? I think you mean, what?' Frankie slinks around Tammy reminding you of a smug cat.

Her lower lip is trembling. Hastily, you open a packet

of chips and offer her a handful. 'Don't listen to him. He's full of it.'

You give Frankie the same look your mum gives your dad whenever the football on tv gets too rowdy, the don't-talk-that-way-in-front-of-children look. Frankie feigns innocence, 'Jessica says all the deaths have been supernatural. Werewolves and vampires ... ghosties and ghoulies.'

Before he can torture Tammy any further, Jessica's voice calls from above, 'Hey guys, come and check this out.'

Frankie's guffaw turns into a whimper but he disguises it by coughing. He's super polite about letting you lead the way up the staircase. Tammy trails after you but you push her back, telling her to wait in the kitchen until you know it's PG. Jessica and Angus stand transfixed in the middle of the hallway staring at an ugly painting of ships. Only it's not the painting they're staring at, it's something built into the wall beside the painting.

'I think there's someone in there.' Angus tilts his head towards the red door perched on a ledge three quarters of the way up the wall. The door has ornate symbols carved into the wooden panels but it's the strange size that perturbs you. It's about half the height of a normal door. There's a wooden ladder perched precariously in the hallway leading up to the door.

Jessica, nose buried in her tablet, is muttering everything from dwarf ghoul to communal hallucination.

Thump. Thump. Thump. Scccrrrrrruuuufffff. Each successive thump seems to be coming closer, as if moving down the wall. You hold your finger up to your lips telling the others to be quiet. Carefully you press your ear against the faded wallpaper. In the silence you hear a rattling sound, slow and controlled, like someone sucking air between their teeth. In. Out. In. Out.

11

'Mummy? Is that you?' someone whispers in your ear. You jerk away from the wall. The others have backed up to the stairs but as leader of the group, you have to show some gumption. You realise it's only someone or something with its mouth pressed up against the other side of the wall.

Your voice comes out as a squeak, 'Um ... no. My name's Drew.'

'The Matron calls us Amelia. So very pleased to meetcha. Can you please let us out?' Her voice is reedy and lilting but it's edging towards sharpness like blowing on a recorder too hard.

'Um ... the door's too high for me to reach.'

'You could stand on the shoulders of one of your little friends.' The voice has moved around to the wall closest to Jessica. She yelps and leaps back onto Frankie's toes. 'If you let me out, I'll help you. Tell you who's killing the kiddies. Tell you how to stop it.'

You decide to let Amelia out (Turn to page 80)

You decide not to let Amelia out (Turn to page 20)

4

Your newfound leadership makes you take a solid step back.

'You're on your own, buddy! Jessica and I didn't steal anything. We'll be fine.'

Angus looks over the edge of the moonbow. In the glow of the lantern, the Ferryman's face appears sallow and his eyes are narrow slits but it's not as intimidating as the cackling leprechaun, lurching towards you. Angus takes one look at the gnomish form and jumps off the bridge. You can't believe he's abandoned you again.

'Uh … Mr Leprechaun?' Jessica's voice is faint. 'We didn't steal anything.' He's twenty steps away. 'We just want to cross to the other side.' Fifteen and now there's a jaunty spring to his step. 'We're really sorry.'

You grab Jessica by the wrist and start running. He's right behind you, chortling and mumbling recipes for children pie.

Faster! Faster! Lift your foot, now the other foot. The

moonbow waxes and wanes. Suddenly Jessica is no longer by your side. There's no time to turn around. The monster is hot on your heels. Thud. Your breath is knocked out of you. You're rolling around on the moonbow, wrestling the dirty knife from his hand. Too late now to jump over the edge. The leprechaun's breath reeks of rotten cabbage as he leers over you. It's over before you know it.

When you wake up, you can hear water slapping against something.

'Where am I?' You feel like you've run a marathon.

The Ferryman draws back his oar and ploughs into the depths. He lowers his hood and you can see the skeletal form underneath. 'Sooner or later, everyone pays the Ferryman.'

(Turn over)

The End
(Return to page 58)

5

Just as you're about to pull back the handle, Jessica puts her hand on your shoulder.

'Are you really sure you want to open the drawer?'

Yes! Yes! Get on with it. Shake off her hand and tell her to stop being such a chicken (Turn to page 38)

Agree with her but you really want to know what's in that drawer dammit! Try and convince Frankie to open it. You don't like him much anyway (Turn to page 24)

Agree with her and step away from that drawer (Turn to page 27)

6

It's not all bad. The rock has a flat surface and a sharp end. It's been fashioned into a makeshift hammer with rope and a wooden handle. It worked for Thor, right? Not that he ever had to battle wicker witches. You weigh the rock hammer in your hands, switching it between the left and the right.

'Bring it on!' You take a few practice swipes relishing the whipping sound the hammer makes as it whisks through the air. The wax has fused your feet to the ground. Any moment now.

Even though Angus and Jessica, those snivelling traitors, have taken the torch you can clearly see the wicker witches staggering towards you. Their feet splay like the tuber roots of a tree – swollen toes, hairs coming out, dirt stuck under the toenails.

They're closing in now. You raise the rock. The wax is hardening across your chest. You can barely flex your torso to swing the handle. They're less than a metre away. With effort, you draw the weapon across your shoulders. The witches smile. They can smell your fear.

You imagine the wax figurine smashing into a million pieces. You drive the rock forward but you're paralysed. You try again. The wax has pinned your arms and is inching its way up your neck. The wicker witches raise their waxy arms to embrace you. As the flames dance across their faces, you realise you've made the wrong choice. Scissors. Always pick Scissors.

THE END
(Return to page 30)

7

Out of the corner of your eye, you can see the others shaking their heads vehemently and making cross signs with their arms.

'No, I really don't think so,' you say firmly. 'We have to go now.'

You have no idea where you're going but anywhere else sounds like a good plan. There's a galumphing sound inside the wall. Amelia is following you down the hall.

'Wait! Can you at least bring me some food? You can leave it by the ledge of the door. If you do, I'll keep watch for you. Warn you when it's coming.'

'What do you eat?' Angus stuffs his trembling hands inside his jacket. You can hear what he's thinking. Fat children's sausage fingers with the nails pulled off, sautéed in butter and garnished with bellybutton fluff.

'Oh chocolates if you please. The Matron locks them

in the third drawer of her desk. Rots the teeth, she says. The key is in the sewing box on top of the bookcase. Her office is just through that door straight ahead.'

You don't have to confer with the others. Some chocolate sounds good right now. The door squeaks when you turn the handle. There's still enough light coming through the bay windows to make out an old-fashioned writing desk in the middle of the room and a grand piano in the corner.

You've learnt from your mum how to read people by the way they keep their workspace. She could take one look at the textbooks strewn across your desk, the scrunched up notepaper and broken pens, and know you were struggling at school. If the textbooks were stacked neatly and the pens were aligned parallel to the books, she'd know you'd only pretended to do your homework.

As you stare at the rotten apple core, the concentric coffee rings, the dead pot plant and the yellow paper with doodles around the margin, the Matron takes form in your head. An older woman, eccentric and erratic, who had her hands full taking care of the kids.

There are some faded photos in frames along the back wall. You blow the dust off the top of the frames and study the photos. The Matron has white hair cut into a neat bob. She's wearing baggy overalls that make her look more wily than skinny. Two toddlers sit on her knees and several older kids hang around her shoulders laughing. You don't recognise the Grecian columns or the paintings in the background. This photo couldn't have been taken in the orphanage.

'Where are you in this photo?' you call to Amelia.

Amelia chortles. 'As if. The Matron never took me on excursions. She only took her pets. The ones who did exactly what she wanted.'

21

You feel a little sorry for her but you're distracted by a terrible twang. Jessica is standing by the piano trying to make out a melody. You wince. When was the last time that piano had been tuned?

'Guys. Come take a look at this.' She's opening up the lid, peering into the piano's belly. Leaving the photos, you stride across the room. You've never seen the inside of a piano but you're pretty sure it shouldn't be a nest of broken wires, the hammers left to hit the exposed wood. You notice that some of the wires are stained a rust colour. There's no point asking Angus his opinion. One look at his blotchy face tells you he'll be blubbering in a minute.

'It looks like a crime scene,' Jessica voices aloud exactly what you're thinking. 'Should we ask Amelia?'

'Idiot! She probably is the killer,' Frankie hisses.

You all turn towards the wall. The tension is broken by a sharp rap close to the bookshelf. You're not sure what Amelia wants to point out. A certain book, perhaps. *Moby Dick* by Herman Melville, *Twenty Thousand Leagues Under the Sea* by Jules Verne, *Encyclopaedia Britannica*. It's hard reading the titles along the spines. Then you see it. A glass box wedged like a bookend against the *Goosebumps* paperbacks. It has an intricate inlay of seashells on the lid. You trace the pattern with your finger to delay opening it. Finally, Frankie rolls his eyes and snatches it from you. Inside are the contents of a sewing kit. Cotton thread. Needles. Pincushion. Scissors.

'Well, that's scary,' Frankie mocks. He hasn't seen the brass key with a red ribbon looped around its bow.

After you fish it out, Amelia gurgles and claps her hands in delight. 'Oh goody good.'

'Just open the drawer so we can get out of here,' Angus

whimpers. You take the key and slide it effortlessly into the keyhole. There's a clicking sound as you release the clasp.

Are you sure you want to open the drawer?

Yes! (Turn to page 17)

No! (Turn to page 27)

8

There's some sense in what Jessica is saying. You pause.

'Whatsa matter?' Frankie taunts. 'Bwak, bwak, bwak, bwak!'

You leave the key in the lock taking a decisive step back. 'I'm not sure this is a good idea anymore.'

'This entire trip to the orphanage was a stupid idea,' Frankie explodes. 'We should be out there hunting the killer. You're the worst leader ever. Get outta my way. I'm in charge now.'

You pull the others back as Frankie hunkers down on his haunches and pulls open the drawer. His piggy eyes are beadier than usual when he's confused. 'What the? Ew!'

A skeletal pair of hands crawl out. Their skin is dried, papery and draped like they've been partially deboned. A second and third pair of hands crawl out. Where the hands have been severed at the wrist, you can see scar nodules from the clumsily knotted flesh. It's pretty creepy so you're surprised when Frankie raises an eyebrow. 'La-ame.'

One of the hands pauses as if offended. As if it had heard. But that's impossible. Hands don't have ears. It waggles one finger at Frankie admonishingly. Then, without warning, it swings to the second drawer and pulls on the handle.

Frankie leaps back but it's too late. Balls are leaping from the drawer. Bouncing balls with slimy trails like half-boiled eggs. Squishy balls like the plastic sort you can buy from vending machines for fifty cents. Only these are not balls. They're eyeballs. Their irises flash an array of violets, blues and greens, their pupils dilated with excitement.

The hand isn't done. It crawls to the third drawer and slides it open with a flourish. Crimson lips rise out like the fresh tips of tulips.

'Oooooooooh,' they chorus as the eyeballs jump towards Frankie.

'Aaaaaaaaaaah,' they sigh as the balls make their way up Frankie's trouser legs and onto his face. The eyeballs mucous tails make wet, slapping sounds. Boing. Schlapp. Boing. Schlapp.

You feel a tingling sensation half way up your leg. There's a hand crawling up your thigh like eensy-weensy spider. You yelp and shake it off but it clings stubbornly and makes a rude gesture. Another hand is clapped over Angus' mouth to stop him from screaming. A third cracks its knuckles and crab walks towards Jessica. You try to help her but you've got your hands full. You're pinned to the wall. Your eyelids are pinched open.

Amelia purrs, 'My, what lovely eyes you had.'

THE END
(Return to page 17)

9

You shake your head as if waking up from a trance. What just happened? Why were you even contemplating opening that drawer? Why in God's name would you trust a creepy, disembodied child voice from within the walls of an abandoned orphanage?

'Everyone get back to the kitchen!' You leave the key in the lock and step away from the desk. A grumbling in your stomach reminds you it's been hours since lunch.

The trail of cookie crumbs lead from the kitchen counter to the front door, and after that, there's no signs of Tammy.

'I told her to wait for us right here.' You can't quite meet Angus' accusing eyes.

'She's probably just gone into the woods to take in the scenery.' Jessica gestures to the view through the door. It's no enchanted woodlands with moss-covered rocks, dangling fuchsias and fairy circles. It's the forest out of a Grimm Brothers'

fairy tale – dark, thorny and home to wolves and other carni-
vores.

'She's probably fed up with your poor leadership.'
Frankie starts mimicking you, 'Let's go to the orphanage instead
of hunting the killer. Let's open the drawer because a creepy
voice told me to. Oh boohoo. I've changed my mind. I'm too
scared to open the drawer.' He folds his arms and sits on the
couch looking mutinous. 'I'm not going out there to look for
her. It's already dark.'

Part of you wants to curl up on the couch next to him
and refuse to budge. On the other hand, you were meant to
keep an eye out for Tammy. Angus is your friend. You can't
let the forest swallow his little sister.

The woods seem a lot more ominous at night. Gnarled branches become arthritic fingers itching to scratch your eyes out.
The rustling leaves are the trees whispering mayhem and
murder.

Angus keeps turning back towards the house, longing
for the warm lights in the window. Once you turn around, but
all you see is Frankie's sneering face misting up the glass.

Jessica breaks off a branch and brandishes it in front
of her as she walks, warding off snakes and beating out a path,
but the track is well worn. Someone else walked this path
recently. You call out Tammy's name a few times.

'Please don't do that,' Jessica begs. 'You never know
what's going to call back.'

Up ahead, the trees form a fortress. Their trunks are
knobbier than usual and their ropey branches are linked hands
you can't cross. After poking around for a few minutes, you
find a small gap to crawl through. You peel back the foliage
so Jessica and Angus can crawl through first.

'Ompf!' Angus has stopped in his tracks causing you to run into him.

'Sorry.'

There's no reply. He's too busy scratching at the peat with both hands. You follow the rustling noise with your torch – dried leaves, rocks and a hand appear in the cone of light. A tiny hand attached to a tiny arm and a tiny body.

Tammy! Angus scoots down to cradle her lifeless body. 'What's happened to her?' he moans. 'Mum's gonna kill me.'

As you try to ease her out of his arms, white flakes stick to your shirt. 'What the?'

You tentatively pick up a flake. It breaks in half. There's more down your front – tacky, white stuff that dries as soon as you notice its gooeyness.

'She's encased in wax!' Jessica pulls you away and starts brushing you down. 'Uh-oh. This is bad.'

It's getting itchy. A large patch has crusted to the front of your jacket and is dribbling down your jeans. 'What's bad?'

Even though you can see the wax crusting to your fingers, you're not panicking. On the contrary, you're overcome by a sense of calmness. You inhale deeply. Mm. Gardenia. Tuberose. Jasmine.

'Relax Jess,' you say dreamily.

'Wicker witches!' She rummages through her backpack, pulls out a peg and clamps it over her nose making her sound like she's blocked up from a cold. 'I've read all about them in *Scented Supernatural.* They lull you into a sense of dullness and kill you.'

'Sandalwood and lavender. My favourite.' Angus seems to have forgotten Tammy lying stiffly at his feet.

The trees are closing in. Shuffling like old people. Dribbling waxy secretions onto the ground with every step. The wax drips and curls into crevices forming eyes, mouths and noses. They look and smell like giant scented figurines from a candle shop.

Jessica pulls out two more pegs and places them on you and Angus. The spell breaks.

'Wicker witches?' Angus howls. 'Let's get out of here!' He grabs the torch, scoops up Tammy's stiffened form and flees.

'Come on, Drew!' Jessica takes off. She's the fastest runner on the track team at school. She used to try and get you to train with her but you always laughed and asked what was so great about being sporty.

You stagger after her but the wax on your jeans has set hard. You hold out your hands to break your fall.

'Wait for me,' you cry, but the words come out muffled. The wax has coated your lips shut. You try yelling out some swear words but realise you're wasting time. You upturn your knapsack looking for a weapon. Rock. Paper. Scissors. What the? You will never let Tammy pack the survival kit again!

What do you choose?

Rock (Turn to page 18)

Paper (Turn to page 40)

Scissors (Turn to page 43)

31

10

'Nice try Amelia.' You fold your arms. 'No more bedtime stories. You owe us a better clue or else …' you pause. What's the worst thing you can do to an orphan spirit?

'We'll eat all your chocolate,' Angus blurts out, his lower lip quivering at the thought.

'Speak for yourself,' Frankie mutters under his breath.

'We'll board up your door so you'll have no chance of getting out ever again,' Jessica suggests.

'We'll go through the adoption records and change your profile so no one will ever, ever, ever want to adopt you,' Frankie offers.

His suggestion is so nasty, it's actually pretty good. There's a sharp intake of breath from the inside of the wall, as if Amelia has swelled up with indignation.

'That's a good idea,' you say loudly, walking over to what looks like a filing cabinet. 'Now where do you think the children's records are kept?'

You open the first drawer. Nothing but cables and electronic plugs. You open the second drawer. Bills and correspondences dating back at least twenty years. You open the third drawer.

'Oh here we are. What did you say your surname was Amelia? Abbotson? Bazeley? Cromwell? Ahhh. Amelia Jenkins. Ten years old. Fluent in English and French. Ooh la la. Let's change that to … speaks only pigeon-English.' You scribble on her file.

'Cut that out! That's private information you're going through. It's illegal.'

'Where did you learn to play the violin?' Jessica asks peering over your shoulder. 'We should change that to the viola.' Seeing Angus' confused expression she adds, 'It's like a violin for kids with no talent. No parents want a kid who plays the viola.'

'Stop it,' Amelia howls.

Amelia's got a record a mile long. You pull out a second and third folder. Geez Louise! How did she have enough time to cause so much trouble?

'September 14th,' you recite, 'Amelia bites Alex Cromwell. Draws blood. Stitches required. Amelia locked up overnight as punishment. September 20th. Sue-Li and Gabbie Thomas missing in woods. Returned by Mr Ferryman (what a nice man he is and so attractive as well). When interrogated separately, both girls claimed Amelia trapped them at the old water well but could not specify how. Amelia locked in wall for three days as punishment. October 20th. Stephen Abbot wakes up with deep bite marks on left thigh and arm. Blood loss. Tetanus shot required. Bite marks consistent with Amelia's teeth. Amelia locked in wall for five days as punishment.'

33

'You're a naughty girl Amelia,' Frankie taunts. 'If you tell us where the Matron is, we'll let you out of the wall.'

'Bite me!' she retorts.

'I'd like to see you try,' Frankie flares up.

'Uh ... guys.' Jessica has opened the fourth drawer and is rifling through the files.

'Let me out of the wall, then we'll see who's so tough.'

'Tell us what happened to the Matron and we'll let you out of the wall.' Frankie sounds smug as if he's just won even though the conversation is going around in a circle.

'Guys shut up for a second,' Jessica yells. 'Look at these other files. They're the ones for the deceased orphans. There's a weird pattern. Look at their medical notes.'

Jessica hands the folder to you to read aloud. 'Freddy Rowland – dental appointment, tooth infection. Both incisors extracted. Donnie Wiley – dental appointment, gum disease. Possible teeth extraction. James Joslin – dental check-up, gum disease. L molar extraction.' It's hard to be heard over the wailing. 'Uh ... Amelia. Who's the dentist that looks after the orphans?'

'Doc Choc, of course.'

The others face expressions mirror your confusion. 'You mean Doc Choc is a doctor? I mean, he's a dentist?'

'Well, I hardly think you can be a doctor of chocolate,' Amelia replies.

'We just thought ... all this time, we thought the lab coat and safety goggles were just for appearance.'

The puzzle pieces are coming together in your head. All this time Amelia denied killing the Matron. And the Ferryman said the Matron wouldn't harm a hair on the children's heads.

'You guys,' you say slowly, 'what if the Matron was

hoarding chocolate to stop the kids from getting cavities so they didn't need the dentist. What if she suspected Doc Choc had a hand in the killings?'

'Of course! It would explain everything.' Jessica hits her forehead with her hand. 'Sally Ellersen was killed eating chocolate. Noel had a chocolate covered booger up his nose. Leah Reiner wasn't at Sally's birthday party because they hated each other. One a slob, the other a health nut. Or so she always claimed. In ballet class, her bun was always immaculate. The only way she could have gotten it that way is if she used a donut to form her bun. A sugared donut that she scoffed down afterwards. Every time she finished ballet, her hair was down.'

'Amelia, was it Doc Choc who killed you?'

You can hear Amelia's sulking through the walls but the thought of you defacing her files wins out. 'The Matron got the kiddies out in time. Mummy they called her. Ha! All her precious babies. She smuggled them to the Ferryman. He was going to take them to the next town and she would have escaped too but then she realised her big mistake. Did a head count. Realised no one had been bitten for a while because I was still locked in the wall. She came back for me but it was too late. Ran into the dentist and then it was bye-bye mummy. I screamed and screamed for weeks to be let out but no one came back. They never came back. So I'm still here.'

It's a terrible story and you're not sure if you swallow all of it. You glance at Jessica who looks as shocked as you feel. She clears her throat. 'That's a terrible thing to happen. If you tell us where Doc Choc's surgery is, we'll make sure the Matron is avenged.'

'Oh, we don't go to him. He comes to visit. Once a month, when the moon is a crescent-shaped fingernail.'

'Like the shape of the moon outside the window right now!' Angus looks like he's going to faint.

Ker-sneeze.

'Bless you,' Jessica says.

'That wasn't me,' you protest.

'Or me,' Angus squeaks.

Ker-thunk. Ker-thunk. Scraaaap.

Amelia lets out a muffled squeak like she's clapped her hand over her mouth. 'He's here. He's coming up the stairs.'

Sure enough heavy boots are treading down the hall-way. Angus pushes Jessica in front of him as a human shield. It's too late to escape. He's right outside the Matron's office. He pauses to scrape his shoes across the scratchy mat and you can't help but think that at least your deaths will be clean at the hands of a dental hygienist.

Click. Squeak squeak.

Doc Choc is a lanky man, bald as a shiny egg with a hooked nose and blue lips drawn in a thin line. His bushy eyebrows knit a straight line across his forehead as he surveys your group. 'What do we have here?'

'No-nothing Doctor,' Angus squeaks.

'Speak up boy! Only children with cavities mumble and grumble.'

Angus makes a break for the door but Doc Choc has arms like rubbery spaghetti ending in pink latex gloves. He grabs Angus by the scruff of his neck and suspends him by his collar from one of the rusted coat hooks nailed to the wall.

Doc Choc's icy eyes rest on Jessica. 'Tut tut. Did you eat chocolate with braces?'

Jessica frantically wipes the chocolate smears from her mouth but it's too late. Out pops his gloved hand from his pocket and the next thing you know, Jessica's swinging by the second hook on the wall, smelling like talcum powder and rubber.

The Doc smiles showing a perfect set of pearly whites like an American tourist. He looks from you to Frankie. 'Who's first?'

'Pssst,' Amelia whispers. 'Let me out. I'll help you.'

Maybe Amelia is your only hope? Let her out (Turn to page 45)

It looks like the end but you're going down fighting. Do not let Amelia out (Turn to page 84)

11

Jessica draws back with a look of hurt in her eyes. You feel bad but instead of apologising, you slide open the drawer. Something leaps onto your face. Your cheeks are burning. You reach up and touch something smooth and hard as a nut.

One look at Jessica's horrified expression and you start screaming, 'Get it off! Get it off!'

You pinch at the nut-shaped creature and hurl it across the room with all your strength. Wisps of spun glass tangle in your hands. Angry welts appear where the fine threads touch your skin.

Thud. Shluuuuurrrrp.

It hits the wall and slides to the floor leaving a black smear on the paisley wallpaper. It looks like a prehistoric beetle, with golden pincers and bronze plates down the length of its body. For a moment, you think it's over. You've killed it. Then, its spiny body rolls over and scuttles towards you. The others scream and leap out of the way. There's no time for bug spray. You grab the scissors from the sewing kit and run towards the creature with a battle cry.

There's a loose nail in the floorboard.

'Ooopfff!

You hold out your hands to break your fall. The scissors drive up into your stomach. As you lie there wheezing and gasping your last breath, you hear a reproachful voice.

'Mummy doesn't like it when you run with the good scissors.'

THE END
Return to page 17

12

The wax has fused your legs together making you shuffle like a Japanese geisha. God knows why you're clutching the bundle of paper. Perhaps you're hoping to write your epithet before you die.

The wicker witches are closing in, wicks on their heads alight. The flames have melted their eyes but you can make out their hooked noses and garish o-shaped mouths.

'Eeeeippp!' In your panic you fling the pile of paper at the wicker witches as they approach.

Frankie's jeering voice resounds in your ear, 'What are you trying to do? Defeat them with paper cuts?'

The paper brushes a wick and catches alight. The wicker witches jolt back. The flames roar with new life. You're surprised by the intensity of the fire until you realise its recycled paper. The high pulp content must make it highly flammable. The witches are melting quickly. And by standing just close enough to the flame, you've melted the wax off your legs without catching alight.

As soon as you have full range of movement, you scamper. North, south, east, west. You don't care which direction you take so long as it's away from here. It's hard to find the path without a torch. You misjudge and take a tumble. Once, you think you recognise a certain tree near the orphanage. It has a distinct u-shaped kink in its branch. When you get closer it's a nest of killer dragonflies. You take off in the opposite direction and don't stop until you reach a clearing. As you pause to catch your breath, you notice the moon shining through the canopy. You've never appreciated how numerous the stars or how brightly they shine when they're not competing against the city lights. For a moment, you stand in silent reverence.

Something sharp grazes your arm. 'Ow.'

Your sleeve is singed. A lump of metal hits the ground near your feet leaving a trail of dust. You bend over to pick it up but it's like picking up a sea urchin. There are no safe spots.

'Ow again.' Another piece finds its mark on your leg, this time drawing blood. As you stare at the spiky lump of glittering metal, you realise it's a falling star. A third piece skids across the dirt, narrowly missing your foot. Perhaps you've stumbled into some sort of cursed fairy field. Jessica would know – she's always got some explanation for the supernatural.

'Drew, get outta there!' Sometimes when you're in high-stress situations, you hallucinate and start hearing voices.

'Run Drew! Run!'

It's Angus and Jessica, hidden by the bushes. Angus even has the spotlight trained on you. As you run for cover, two more flaming shurikens fly by. One grazes your ear and the other spears a fluffy bunny nearby, grazing on grass and minding its own business. Jessica's hands reach out and pull you under the canopy.

'What was that?' you pant.

'A mystical meteor shower. So unlucky. We usually don't see them this time of the year. I read all about them in *Mystical Meteorological Manifestations*. Of course, there are worse things to be caught in.'

'Like wicker witches?' You can't keep the caustic tone out of your voice. You're burnt, bruised and bleeding while Jessica and Angus have probably been picnicking all this time. They exchange a look and you feel a stab of jealousy. They deserted you. You risked your life to save Tammy and they were too scared to help you.

A moment ago you wanted to hug them but now you're thinking they both deserve to die.

How could they have left you like that? They totally deserve to die (Turn to page 50)

On the other hand, they may come in handy in the future and now that you have a torch, you have a better chance of getting back to the house. Forgive and forget (Turn to page 56)

13

You frantically peel the wax from your legs. You can feel the wax under your fingernails, crawling up your neck and creeping inside your ears. Even though you know you'll soon be completely paralysed, there's a soothing warmness to it.

In the moonlight, you see the wicker witches staggering closer. Their arms are part tree bark, part flesh and make a horrible crunching sound like bones knitting together as they reach for you. The wicks on their heads are alight.

The wax has fused your feet to the ground. This is your last stand. You grab the scissors and brace yourself to stab the closest witch. They're closing in now. Their waxy faces are lit up with glee as they raise their arms to encase you. You pull your arm back and drive the scissors straight into a witch's heart. You have excellent aim but alas, they are blunt-tipped training scissors, not even sharp enough to cut through cardboard. The wax is inching up your face and into your nostrils.

It's coating your eyelashes. You stop struggling. You feel like a donut, warm and doughy, peering out at the world through vanilla glaze. You're vaguely aware of the witches gathering around you. One of them is attaching a tapered piece of rope to the top of your head. Another witch presses her forehead against yours initiating you into the group. When she draws back, your wick is glowing warm.

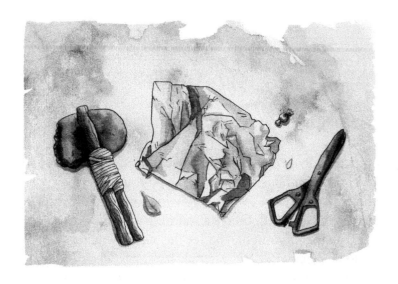

THE END
(Return to page 30)

14

As Doc Choc approaches he scrapes the wallpaper with a silver dental pick making a sound like fingernails down a blackboard. Frankie throws a punch but Doc Choc sidesteps. His torso swings out of the way like a cartoon character made of rubber.

The key to the wall must be the same key that opened the chocolate drawer. It's no longer in the lock. You must have dropped it after the chocolate binge. Can you find it without the Doc seeing? He's got his hands full strapping Frankie to a leather chair. You drop to your hands and knees. The Doctor steps out of the room, whistling as he walks. You run your hands over the soft carpet frantically searching for something unnatural, a piece of metal poking out of the weave.

'What the hell are you doing? Help me,' Frankie hisses.

There's no time. The Doctor returns pulling a trolley along with him. If he looks around now, he'll have you up on a hook too. Your hand closes on something cold and smooth. You can't believe your luck. Clutching the brass key in your palm, you scramble underneath the desk.

There's a small gap between the bottom of the desk and the floor. Doc Choc only has to scrutinise the room to see the bottom of your feet but he seems content to be playing with his tools. You peer through the space. There's the rusty wheels of the trolley. On the bottom shelf are wads of dental pads, blue on one side and white on the other. The sort the dentist tells you to spit up on at the end of treatment but they never absorb the blood. On the next shelf up, there's a pile of rusty tools; hooks, grapplers, loops and dental sticks. The trolley blocks most of Frankie from view but you can see his feet flailing and hear him gurgling as he fights the saliva sucking tube. The Doc turns to face Frankie. Now's your chance.

Knowing there's only seconds to act, you dash over to the wall. Your hand slips once, twice. On the third go, you find your mark. The black hole, the secret in the wall. The key catches and you think it's a mistake. It's not the right key. You try again and hear a sweet click. The wall swings open.

Doc Choc swirls around, the saliva sucker in one hand, a grappling hook in the other. He scratches at his forehead with the grappling hook, leaving a deep cut. No one's made a sound but somehow you hear organ music. Deep pipes bellowing doom. Whose you're not exactly sure.

She appears as slowly as a queen doing a favour for her subjects. One bony foot placed in front of the other. Amelia is all skin and bones, literally. She's so fragile you wonder how you could have been scared of her. There are chunks of rotting flesh flapping from her cheekbones and when she opens her mouth – you nearly faint. Amelia doesn't just have one set or two sets, she has three sets of top teeth.

46

'Give me back my teeth!'

Doc Choc isn't at all fazed by Amelia's appearance. He peers at her through his wireframe glasses and blinks as if he doesn't quite recognise her. 'Ah of course. Amelia Jenkins. Born with a full set of beautiful teeth. Extraordinary. Never seen anything like it and my dear, I've been practising legally for twenty years and illegally for ten. Removed your first incisor when you were five years old. Remarkably early to lose a milk tooth but within two days another perfect tooth appears. When that tooth fell out a year later, a third tooth descended within days.'

Lost in memory lane, the Doc slowly draws each of his four fingers into his palm and forms a fist as if he's still clutching her precious teeth. 'Hyperdontia is extremely rare and usually only one or two teeth. But you were extraordinary. The more I pulled out, the more you grew. What a good team we were.'

'Give me back my teeth!' Amelia roars and charges.

The Doc raises his saw and swings it in a wide arc. Amelia ducks the blow, grabs his arm and forces it backwards. The afterlife has imbued her with super strength because the Doc is forced onto his knees, the torque bending his arm to breaking point. Snap.

Amelia grins as the Doc screams. For a moment you can see the cheeky kid dancing in the skeleton. She drags her prize towards the wall.

'Help me,' the Doc screams. No one moves. You're inclined to throw in his dental tools for Amelia's pleasure as the wall swallows them up. You rush over to unhook Jessica and Angus.

Jessica blocks her ears. From the walls there's a sickening crunching of bones and muffled screaming. 'Let's get out of here.'

48

'Herrrooooo – I can't moorve my mrouth,' Frankie drools waving to get attention. 'I nee hell here.'

At this moment, even Frankie's crankiness can't wipe the smile from your face. You've solved the mystery and stopped the murderer. As you and Angus work to untie the straps, you want to dance a jig. You want to pack your bags and go home. You want to take a shower and jump in your own bed. You want to—

'Something's not right.' Jessica is frowning. She's got that slightly constipated look she gets when solving quadratic equations. 'Where are Amelia's teeth?'

'Huh?'

'The teeth we found in the chocolate. They were only one adult set. The Matron's. Where are Amelia's teeth?'

'He's probably stashed them somewhere else,' Angus suggests, losing the little colour he has regained. 'You're overthinking.'

'We can leave now and never know for sure. Or we can find all the missing teeth and end it for good. We just need to piece together all the clues.'

She's looking at you again. Sigh. In years to come, you know this is the reason you don't try out to be prefect or school captain or any role of responsibility.

End this! Turn to page 86.

15

It's survival of the fittest. If the situation had been reversed, you'd have done the same thing. But you still can't believe they left you.

Angus stops to re-adjust Tammy, who he's carrying across his shoulder. You step on his heel.

'I said I'm sorry. I panicked alright? I didn't realise you weren't behind me.' Angus' lower lip is trembling. Anyone looking at him would think he had almost been turned into a candle.

'And I didn't realise your shoe was in my path,' you reply.

'How'd you escape the wicker witches anyway?' Jessica asks in a small voice. You give them a blow-by-blow description of how you used the paper to start a fire that melted the witches.

'Fight fire with fire,' Jessica repeats. 'Of course! When

50

we get back to the house, we should light the fireplace and melt the wax from Tammy.' Angus' face lights up at the suggestion.

There's a jaunt in your step and you square your shoulders like a brave leader. When Angus turns right on the path, you correct him.

'I'm pretty sure we turn right,' he protests.

'Coming from you who got lost and spent the past hour cowering in tree roots, that's not really much to go on.' You veer to the left leaving them standing indecisively at the junction. After a quick conferral, which annoys you even more because they've become so buddy-buddy, they run after you.

On this side of the forest, the trees are denser. Pine needles prick your arms every time you stumble off the track. You flash the torch over the thicket, trying to retrace your steps, trying to find something sinister from your earlier forage.

Finally, you find the landmark you're after. The u-shaped bend in the tree. The upside-down hive, looking like it's spun from zombie hair, tucked snugly in the crook. It's directly ahead of you. You glance at Angus and Jessica who are too busy looking at each other to have noticed. Good riddance to both of them.

'Hey Angus. I think we're lost. Can you climb that tree? Try and see the orphanage?'

Buzzzzzzzzzzzzzz. You're surprised Angus hasn't noticed the noise. It's distinctly different from the chirruping of crickets, bird songs and other bumps in the night. He's scaling the tree quickly, his hands finding all the right notches, his feet knowing exactly where to plant to distribute his weight.

'What can I do?' Jessica asks.

'You just stand right in that spot and keep an eye out for wicker witches,' you say sweetly. 'And … er … my feet are sore. I'm going to go and sit down by that tree.'

'I can't see much from here,' Angus hollers. 'Too many trees blocking the view.'

You point to where the hive is hidden. 'Get up on that branch. A bit more to the left.'

He steps onto the branch, testing its weight carefully. His fingertips brush the hive. You rub your hands together in anticipation.

Snap! The branch cracks. The hive starts to fall. Angus reaches up and grabs an overhanging branch. As he swings his legs up, he kicks the hive. It flies through the air in a perfect arch, not towards Jessica whose standing directly underneath, but towards you.

Buzzzzzzzzzz. A storm of silver bodies rise as one prickly mass. You raise your arms to cover your face but they're

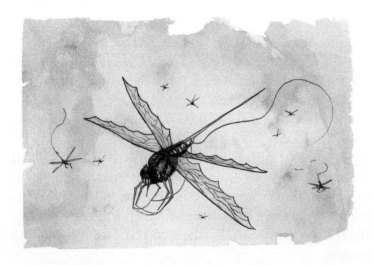

swarming over you. In the moonlight, they look like dragon-flies but close up you can see they are actually sharp needles. They beat their blue-tipped wings persistently against you, looking for exposed skin to attack. You beat some off success-fully but they keep coming back for more. From their abdomens, there's a trail of sticky black thread.

'Aaaarrggg mmmmmm!' You try to open your mouth to scream but they've sewn your lips together.

'Mmmuuummpppgggh!' You try to call for help but Jessica's fled again and Angus is too far up to hear. Your neck is swelling. You've had an allergic reaction. Death is swift but silent.

THE END
(Return to page 42)

16

You hold up your hands in a gesture of surrender. 'Ok, I get that you're pretty mad. But I'm all grown up now and I don't need you anymore.'

Jessica groans and shakes her head. 'What he means to say is, he'll always need you but sometimes kids just need a little space. We're teenagers. You know how we are. Surly.'

'That's right. And it's pretty uncool for a twelve-year-old boy to be talking to a manga character.' Frankie's voice trails off as she looms over us.

'You left me Drew. Do you know what that feels like? No you can't because you have no imagination. Couldn't even imagine a better outfit for me. Look at this black dress. Look at these buttons. I'm the most uncool manga character ever!'

Her blade hand twitches. Any minute she'll be slicing you from ear to ear.

You're backed up against the wall now. You sense Amelia's

54

MARIANNA SHEK

presence on the other side. 'We could use a little help right now if you're not too busy,' you hiss.

'What for? She's only a figment of your imagination.' Amelia sounds surprised.

That's it! You just have to stop thinking about her.

'You didn't teach me how to read or write so I was illiterate and bored waiting for you to come home every day.' Miss Mary Mack descends upon you, silver knife flashing.

Not thinking about her is easier said than done. Especially as the eight foot fury descends upon you and your friends. The rest ... it's up to your imagination.

THE END
(Return to page 63)

17

'Well it hasn't exactly been a picnic for us either,' Angus snaps. You notice a shiner coming up under his left eye and his dishevelled hair is covered in a fine layer of – you're not exactly sure what.

'It's glitter. There's a swarm of pixies up ahead.' Angus claws at his hair to get rid of the excess. 'It could be worse. They hit Jessica right in the face.'

Jessica removes her glasses to show her red and swollen eyes. 'Lucky I wear glasses. Pixie dust makes you blind.'

You open your mouth and shut it immediately, not sure what you were going to say. Something has dissolved between the three of you and there's no need to say anything after all. Working together, it doesn't take long to figure out how to get back to the orphanage. A warm feeling spreads through your body.

As you follow the sloped path down the hill, there's a

drop in temperature. Your boots make a loud, crunching sound as if you're walking on crushed shells or gravel. You've reached the river. The moon casts streaks of rippling light across its surface. A rainbow stretches across the riverbeds like a magical bridge. It is picture perfect, like something out of a fantasy landscape painting. You're about to point it out to the others, but Jessica beats you to it.

'Omigod! It's a moonbow!' She punches your arm.

'You mean … a rainbow?'

'No, I mean a moonbow. It's another mystical meteorological manifestation.'

Something catches your eye – a gnomish man asleep at the base of the moonbow. It could just be a homeless person but given your luck this evening, you know it's something sinister. 'And that would be a leprechaun, I suppose?'

Jessica nods and holds a finger to her lips. 'It's lucky he's asleep. If we can cross the moonbow, it'd be a much shorter route to the orphanage.'

Up close, the leprechaun looks nothing like the happy-go-lucky trickster in pictures. He's more troll than gnome. His large stocky body is curled around a pot filled with golden nuggets. Your fingers feel itchy.

Your foot sinks a little as you step onto the moonbow. It's like walking on marshmallows. You take a second step. The moonbow seems to hold your weight.

The leprechaun grunts mid-snore and mumbles, 'Forty-seven, forty-eight, forty-nine.' He exhales loudly. You gesture for Jessica and Angus to follow.

It's freezing. Every time you step through the mist, your feet turn to icicles. You're pretty sure your socks are soaked through.

'Fifty, fifty-one, fifty-two.'

You're halfway. If you weren't so frightened, you'd stop to admire the view. The river below is an inky blue, dark and brooding. There's movement followed by splash, plop. All you catch are the ripples fanning over the surface as something disappears beneath the water.

'There's someone down there,' Jessica whispers. The mist clears revealing the silhouette of a shrouded figure. He's standing on the bow of a rickety wooden boat, slowly pushing a paddle through the water. Maybe he hasn't seen you. He'll row right under the moonbow. You hold your breath.

He fumbles at something and you see him illuminated in the lantern light. A gaunt, wizened ferryman.

He looks up at the three of you and frowns. 'You kids come down from there. Don't you know the leprechaun will eat anyone who takes his gold? I'll take you safely across the river for a gold coin. Lean over the edge and jump down. I'll catch you.'

'No thanks,' you call back in a loud whisper. 'We don't have any money.'

An angry roar cuts through the mist. 'Ninety-nine! Who's stolen my gold?' The moonbow rocks and shakes as heavy footsteps lumber towards you. Angus fumbles at his pockets scattering a fistful of nuggets.

'You idiot!' Jessica yells.

'Don't let him eat me,' Angus begs. 'Let's go with the Ferryman.'

'I don't have a good feeling about this,' you warn.

You accept a ride from the Ferryman (Turn to page 64)

You don't accept a ride from the Ferryman (Turn to page 14)

MARIANNA SHEK

18

You're pretty sure concealed between the hard covers are wings from dead moths or instructions written in blood on how to bottle the sound of fingernails down a blackboard. Cautiously, you remove the book from the shelf.

'*How to Best Little Beasties*,' Amelia chortles. 'Read it aloud Drew. Go on.'

You don't like Amelia's clues but you flick through the book. There are illustrations of beasts and monsters with complicated diagrams of their weak points. You notice there's a passage on killing wicker witches.

'What's that?' Jessica asks pointing to a dog-eared page.

You flip to the middle of the book and clear your throat.

'I crept and crawled.
You were primed and ready.
You kept me small
while I kept steady.

59

CHOOSE YOUR OWN DEATH

Now I'm the blackest of nights
and the bitterest of greens.
Your sleight of hand
is the red that I've gleaned.
You were tricksy and turvy,
such whirl winding fun.
Now I'm topsy and swervy
and the fun's just begun.'
Jessica takes over the second verse.
'Be still. Stay near.
Your voice rang hollow.
Come now. Come here.
Like a dog I follow.
I watched your back, ol' twinkle toes,
you had a knack for trippin'.
But 'twas I who hooked the garden hose
under your feet while you were skippin'.
And when you lost your baby teeth
you put it down to science.
But while you slept, I pulled them out
with surgical appliance.
So goodbye, goodnight, good-riddance
this is how it's going to end.
Next time think twice before you cross
your imaginary friend.'

You're not sure how the others interpret this but Jessica has a blazing look in her eyes. 'That's it, isn't it? Someone's imaginary friend is killing all the kids.'

'I don't have an imaginary friend,' Frankie snickers. 'How old are you again? Five.'

'Maybe Tammy unleashed it?' you suggest.

'Puh-lease. Tammy was the one who told me Santa Claus

60

isn't real,' Angus shakes his head in disgust.

'Kids these days have no imagination,' Jessica snaps. 'Remember Drew, you used to have an imaginary friend when we were young.'

You feel heat rising in your face. 'I did not.'

'Yeah you did.' Angus snaps his fingers. 'What was her name again? You cried because I accidentally sat on her on the school bus when we went on an excursion in grade three.'

'Oh yeah,' Frankie taunts a mean smile playing on his lips. 'She hated you. She told me.'

'She did not,' you snap. 'Miss Mary Mack was super fun. More fun than you dorks. And she's not a killer.'

'We just need to make sure.' Jessica comes between you and Frankie. 'How do you summon her again?'

'I don't remember.'

'You do!'

Feeling like the biggest fool, you and Angus stand facing each other a stride apart. You've got your back to Frankie but you can feel his smirk as you start clapping hands in unison.

'Miss Mary Mack, Mack, Mack

All dressed in black, black, black

With silver buttons, buttons, buttons.'

Jessica gasps. Out of the corner of your eye you see a faint outline, a tall willowy girl in a black dress with silver buttons down her back.

'Keep going guys,' Jessica urges.

You finish the song and Miss Mary Mack is standing there, a tight lip smile giving nothing away. What are you meant to say after all this time? Hi Miss Mary Mack. Killed any kiddies lately? Somehow you don't think that will go down

well. You remember taking turns swinging from an old tyre your dad strung up on a tree branch overlooking the river. And playing dolls underneath the porch when it got too hot in the summer. Ancient history, before you met Jessica and Angus who told you only little kids play with dolls.

'Hello there Drew,' Miss Mary Mack says ever so sweetly. 'Like my silver buttons?'
She draws a silver blade from the folds of her skirt. 'Got myself a knife to match.'

'Oh boy, I wish Drew hadn't summoned you,' Frankie groans.

Run away. Now (Turn to page 69)

Try to reason with her (Turn to page 54)

19

As the leprechaun lunges, you leap into the air remembering at the last minute you're scared of heights. Oooomppffff. You land feet first in the boat and take a wild step sideways to regain your balance. Thump. Thump. Jessica and Angus land beside you. The boat lurches and you're sure it's going to capsize but the Ferryman steadies it with a bony hand. Angus and Jessica sit on the back seat, furthest away from the Ferryman. You would love to join them but Tammy is wedged between them. You're forced to perch precariously on the bow.

The Ferryman pockets the gold nuggets and chuckles as the leprechaun shakes his fist from above. 'Nice night for a pleasure cruise.'

'Can't you hurry up Sir?' Angus licks his upper lip nervously.

'Relax. It's fading.' The Ferryman points behind you and sure enough, the moonbow has become so transparent, its lost most of its colour. The leprechaun looks no more than a harmless hologram. 'Where are you kids headed?'

'To the orphanage,' Angus pipes up. You throw him a dirty look. There's no need to give away so much information. The Ferryman is still pretty creepy.

'I remember the Matron and her kids.' He scratches at his stubble. 'Once a month I used to row them to the markets in the next town. Five kids in the back, three in the front, the two little ones on the Matron's lap. They made so much ruckus. There was one little girl, Amelia. She was the most trouble of all. Almost made us capsize once or twice.'

He's chuckling as if an unplanned dip into river scum with leprechauns and god knows what else, maybe piranhas, would be the best adventure ever. 'I suppose you kids must have eaten all the cookies and milk I left out? I'll bring more up to the house next week.'

'Oh was that you who has been leaving the food?' Jessica exclaims. 'Thanks but we brought up our own supplies.'

'You kids are prepared. Good.' He scrutinises Jessica from beneath the hood and she blushes. 'Since the Matron's disappearance, it's the least I can do to look after any strays.'

'What happened to the Matron and the kids?' You give Jessica a meaningful look. He'd mentioned Amelia. Could he be referring to your creepy friend in the wall?

The Ferryman adjusts his hood so you can't see his eyes. He takes his time answering. 'You just be careful up at the orphanage. There are some who say the Matron killed them kiddies but I knew her, she wouldn't harm a hair on their heads.'

'What happened to her?' Jessica repeats a little shrilly. The boat hits the sandbank but no one stands up. Finally, Angus lifts Tammy over his shoulder and clambers out of the boat. Jessica trails behind him and you're the last to leave.

'There are some who say the Matron never left the orphanage. If you ask me, find the Matron you'll find the murderer.' The Ferryman pushes his oar off the embankment leaving behind an echo etched into your brain

'Find the Matron you'll find the murderer ... murderer ... murderer.' Only it's not an echo reverberating through the night air, but Angus repeating the mantra under his breath.

'Cut it out!'

Angus trots along the path. 'He's got a point. Maybe we should do a thorough search of the house when we get back. Or we could just ask Amelia.'

Talking to the disembodied voice in the wall again is the last thing you want to do. You can tell Jessica isn't keen either by the way she abruptly changes the subject. 'I hope Frankie's got the fire going and made us dinner.'

You doubt it but you also don't expect him to have boarded up the door so that you have to climb in through a window.

'Well, you guys took so long I thought you were dead,' he explains. No doubt that was why he ate all of the party pies as well. He points to Tammy. 'Great leadership Drew. What happened to her?'

'Shut up and help get some firewood!' Jessica snaps, 'We'll melt the wax off Tammy the same way Drew escaped the Wicker witches.'

Pretty soon there's a roaring fire. You can't help shuddering as the wax melts away like an evil chrysalis and Tammy emerges, disorientated and crying. Jessica pulls and scratches at the exoskeleton until it is completely shed.

'Don't run away again.' Angus breathes a sigh of relief.

'What happened?' Tammy quavers.

Where to begin? It's too much effort even to open and shut your mouth to relay the story. 'We'll tell you about it in the morning. Right now, we're exhausted. Let's go to bed.'

The dormitory has ten bunk-beds in a row. Plenty of room for your group of runaways. Even though you're exhausted, you're not dumb enough to let the others sleep unguarded. As leader, you take the first shift.

Tucked up snug in her blanket, Tammy looks like a soft molehill heaving in and out. Frankie tosses from side to side, occasionally mumbling about eyeballs and hands. Angus has carefully tucked his blanket around him like a sleeping bag all the way up to his ears. Probably afraid if any part of his body is sticking out, the monster under the bed might drag him down.

You're getting very sleepy. Your eyes are barely open. But you have to stay awake. There's someone you need to speak to. Frankie's steady snoring fills you with envy. It's been an exhausting day and, you sniff your armpit, you didn't even get to shower.

There's a soft crooning within the walls, a dulcet voice singing,

'Five little children trapped in a dream
No one's 'round to hear them scream
Rock-a-bye, sleep awhile, we can wait
Soon he'll come and swallow the bait.'

You cup the walls with both hands as if whispering in its ear. 'There's something I've got to ask you. Where's the Matron?'

'We ain't saying nothing more without a treat first,' Amelia shoots back without missing a beat. 'We want the chocolate that's hidden in the locked drawer in Mummy's office.'

'You can't eat chocolate this close to bedtime. Don't you know it'll rot your teeth?' It's something your mum says all the time. You don't believe a word of it but you'd say anything to stall her.

'That's what Mummy said all the time. Like she was concerned. Ha! She just wanted to keep all the chocolate for herself. Ha! And if any of the children tried to steal the key, she'd punish them. Dragged them to her office and whipped them with the piano strings until their flesh bled. I heard their screams.'

'Did the Matron kill the children?'

There's silence. You imagine Amelia's got her hands clamped over her mouth to stop from giggling. She's gnawing on a secret that probably tastes better than chocolate. 'We want the chocolate that's hidden in Mummy's locked drawer in the study. We'll tell you all about Mummy if you get it for us.'

You wouldn't trust Amelia as far you can throw her. You're going nowhere. No one is dying on your shift, soldier. Grab a softball bat and stand tall (Turn to page 72)

You imagine how popular you'll be if you solve the mystery before sunrise. Go to the Matron's office and get Amelia the chocolate (Turn to page 75)

20

For a boy of his considerable mass, Angus can run fast. You're hot on his heels as he rounds the corner and flies down the stairs into the common room. He starts closing the double wooden doors in your face.

'Ooopppff. Wait for the others!'

'Oh yeah. Sorry.'

Jessica and Frankie slide through. You work as a team barricading the door with the couch, heavy coffee table and television set.

Scraaatcch. Scraaaatch. Scraaaatch. You peek through the keyhole. Miss Mary Mack is fuming. She's gnashing her teeth as she grinds the knife against the door panel.

Frankie points an accusing finger in your direction. 'You need to make better friends.'

'When she's on your side, she's great at scaring off bullies,' you explain defensively.

'Yeah, well too bad about her being a serial child killer!'

The door handle rattles with impotent rage. Jessica blocks her ears with both hands. 'Do you think Miss Mary Mack actually killed all the kids? And the Matron? What would be her motivation? Seems to me she's really only after Drew.'

'Thanks a lot!'

Frankie rolls his eyes. 'So what are you saying? Goultown is big enough for two crazy murderers?'

'Amelia said she didn't kill anyone,' Jessica argues.

'Oh, well if the resident Emily LeStrange says she didn't kill anyone, it must be true. You are so naïve.' Frankie rolls his eyes again.

Bam. Miss Mary Mack is charging the door. Angus falls off the couch but otherwise the barricade is holding up well.

'Shut it,' Jessica shouts banging her fist against the door. She turns back to Frankie. 'I'm sick of the way you're always putting everyone down. It's not like you have a better suggestion.'

You hate to agree with Frankie but it does make the most sense. 'Amelia has a good reason for hating the Matron. She was hoarding all the chocolates and whipping the kids ... probably to death.'

'In detective stories there's always a red herring,' Jessica says stubbornly.

Bam. Bam. The television cord unravels and hits her on the head but she doesn't seem to notice.

'You didn't seem so sure when you were begging Drew not to let her out of the wall,' Frankie taunts.

'I'm just saying, let's not jump to conclusions. I didn't say we should let her out of the wall. What about the other children? Sally Ellerson? Noel the Nosepicker? Leah Reiner?

Why would the Matron or Amelia kill them?'

'Shut up,' Angus intervenes.

'You shut up. I can't believe you're taking his side—'

'Shut up!' Angus says again and gesticulates towards the door.

You cock your head to the side. 'I hear nothing.'

'Exactly.'

You summon the courage to peek through the keyhole. Nothing. Except four rounded, silver buttons and a knife lying on the carpet.

'That's it!' You throw your arms around Jessica. 'I remember how I got rid of her when I was younger. You have to ignore her. She can't stand being ignored. Jessica, you're a genius.'

'Yeah well … I had help.' Jessica narrows her eyes at Frankie.

'Duh. I was antagonising you on purpose,' Frankie sneers. 'Well done team.'

He raises his hand to high five her but Jessica turns away. You don't like to leave people hanging. After all, you're in this together. You slap his palm – a bit harder than necessary. He shakes his hand smarting from the blow. It's time to head back to the Matron's office and catch up with that trickster Amelia. This time, you won't be fooled.

Go back to the office
(Turn to page 32)

21

You ignore Amelia's pleas for chocolate. She sulks and tries to hook you with more cryptic messages about the Matron. You pace back and forth, lightly gripping a softball bat over one shoulder. Amelia is not helping. She's given up and has turned her attention to rattling the pipes in the walls and singing softly,

'Tat. Tut-a-tut. Just the shutters my dear.

The bumps in the night, that's what you can hear.'

Something flickers in the corner. You shine your torch into the darkness, running the light over every nook and cranny. Just the silhouette of a tree branch outside. You have half a mind to turn on the lights and wake everyone up but they'll think you're chicken.

'Behind the curtains, what's lurking there?

With morning breath and grizzled hair?'

You can't help shining your torch over the gossamer veil.

Why do curtains always look like ghostly apparitions? Goose bumps slowly spread over your arms and the back of your neck. Someone's watching you. You're sure of it. Standing in the middle of the room makes you an easy target. It's so exposed. There's a spare bed next to Jessica. You can still keep watch from there and you'll be a lot safer wrapped under the blankets where it can't see you.

'Shush and a hush. Go to sleep instead.

No need to rush. It's not under the bed.'

You can feel your eyes drooping as you snuggle into the pillow. Mm. Fresh linen. Soft, downy pillows. The torch slips from your grip and angles crazily where the beam hits the ceiling.

Snort. Grunt. Your eyes fly open. You're having a heart attack. You struggle to rise. There's something heavy on top of you.

'Murrrrgggggghhhh!' Your scream comes out a feeble cry. Your hand closes around the torch and you aim it upwards.

Green like an ogre. Flat nose flaring at the nostrils like an electric socket. Black wine gums for teeth. Pustules on its chin with hairy bits poking out. Its hair, like twigs on a broomstick, is tied in place by a handkerchief. It's a hag. Sitting cross-legged on your chest, filing its gnarly toenails with a dirty knife.

'Mmmmurrrgggh!' You expect Jessica's eyes to fly open but she's fast asleep. You thrash madly and the hag grins her black wine gums at you. She leans in close. The last thing you hear is Amelia's sing song voice,

'Nyeh he he hee. It's on my chest.

Just close your eyes. It's time to rest.'

THE END
(Return to page 68)

22

The Matron's office is even creepier at night. The high ceiling with its exposed wooden beams is perfect for nesting bats, vultures or other winged beasts to swoop down on their victims. You walk towards the desk giving the piano a wide berth but it's not enough to stop the images creeping into your peripheral vision of screaming children whipped with wire.

The sewing box with its lid gaping open is on the desk as you left it. The Victorian style brass key is still jutting into the keyhole of the top drawer. You pause to examine the intricate pattern carved into the head. The crevices that form the swirling patterns are stained with rust or maybe blood. Whatever it is, someone tried to polish out the evidence because the rest of the key is a dull gold sheen. The key to the chocolate drawer must have been a valuable prize for the orphans. Maybe the Matron looped the key around a belt that she wore at all times to stop the kids from trying to steal it.

Somehow Amelia's account of the Matron doesn't fit with the Ferryman's, but who's lying?

You have an ominous feeling of déjà vu. Every part of you repels against opening the drawer but it seems you've got no choice. Behind the wall, Amelia chortles and claps her hands with glee.

Click. It's a prehistoric beetle with pincers sharp as knives. It's a pair of severed hands gesturing rudely. It's a jostle of squishy eyeballs bouncing across the floor leaving a trail of gooey mucous. It's the end.

You rear back instinctively in horror, hands covering your face. Just as the beetle is set to drill its pincers into your yielding flesh, an image flashes across your mind. The Ferryman stamps on the prehistoric bug, bats away the eyeballs with his oar and uses a hand gesture on the severed hands that sends them scuttling back to the drawer.

'It's not your turn to cross, boss.' He salutes you and the vision disappears.

You look in the drawer again. You must need your eyes tested. There are no prehistoric beetles or eyeballs – just slabs of Doc Choc Chocolate in shiny, purple foil. You remember that Doc Choc used to donate boxes of candy to the kids at the orphanage for Christmas and Easter. This must have been where the Matron stored them.

'The fruit and nut slab is my favourite,' Amelia reminds you of your promise. 'You can slide it under the door.'

You're on the verge of asking what door when you see an unnatural line running down the length of the wallpaper and another line where the wall should be flush against the carpet. There's a secret door in the wall! This must be the other end of the passageway that starts with the door in the middle of the wall. You run your hand over the wallpaper until

it hits a dint. You marvel at the trick of light, the perfect cam-
ouflage, the tiny keyhole hidden in the floral centre of the
wallpaper. It looks the same size as the fancy brass key you
fitted into the chocolate drawer.

Luckily the bar of chocolate is thin enough to slide
under the crack of the door. Amelia grabs it from the other
side before you've pushed the entire slab through and you jerk
your hand away. There's the sound of foil tearing and a satisfy-
ing crunch as Amelia devours the treat.

'My turn now. Where's the Matron?'

'I-almurghdy-given-youmurhghghghg-oooohh.' She
must have stuffed the whole block in her mouth at once.

'Say it again?'

'I said I've already given you the clue.'

'You have not.'

'Go look in the drawer again,' Amelia insists.

There's nothing there but chocolates. Caramel swirls,
pistachio nougat, peanut butter brittle, fruit and nuts.

'Help yourself,' Amelia purrs in a perfect hostess tone.

You don't like where this is going but your stomach
growls. It's not like you've had dinner. Before you dig in, you
decide to wake the others, well except Tammy. She's had enough
adventure for one night and needs to rest. The others can help
work out Amelia's cryptic clue.

Jessica's awake in a flash, glasses on, tablet tucked under
one arm. Angus and Frankie stumble bleary-eyed into the
study. Angus is mumbling about wicker witches and Frankie
slumps into a chair, showing his resentment by yawning point-
edly. His eyes light up though when you show him the chocolate.

'Be careful. They may be poison—' Jessica warns. Too
late. He's ripped open the wrapper and stuffed a row of peanut

butter brittle into his mouth. Angus watches Frankie like a hawk as if expecting him to pass out.

Frankie burps loudly. 'The peanut butter brittle's the best.'

Jessica turns to you and shrugs. Soon you're all indulging in Doc Choc's generosity. The Matron must have hoarded all the chocolate donations for herself, never giving any to the kids. You're almost glad the greedy woman disappeared.

'Try the caramel swirl.' Jessica breaks off a row and passes it to you.

'I like the white chocolate nut best,' Angus says.

You turn your head sideways to read the torn wrapper from his bar. 'Angus you've got a praline bar. There are no nuts. What are you talking about?'

'What are these white pieces then?' Angus asks, waving the bar in your face.

The others peer over your shoulder as you delicately dislodge a nutty shard from the chocolate centre. Jessica prods it with a finger flipping it on its side. She pinches it between index finger and thumb and holds it up to the light. It's a calcified rock, a little yellow along the cracks but definitely a tooth. A molar to be precise.

You spit out the rest of the chocolate. 'Ewwwwwwww. Vomit!'

'Oh disgusting!' Angus swallows his mouthful quickly, afraid of being judged.

'Gross out!' Frankie runs out of the room. He returns with several bottles of soft drink and a few plastic cups. Jessica gargles furiously while you extract several more teeth from the chocolate bar.

'Never mind the teeth. The chocolate's still good. It's within the expiry date and the Matron always said calcium is good for your bones,' Amelia says soothingly.

'That's not funny Amelia,' you snap. 'And you still haven't told us where the Matron is.'

As soon as you say it, you get a sickening feeling you know the answer. Frankie refuses to go anywhere near the chocolate, but between you, Jessica and Angus, you pull apart the rest of the blocks. The teeth are scattered like prizes in a sandpit. You manage to extract a full set of adult dentures.

'Poor, poor Mummy,' Amelia croons.

What sort of sicko is she? What sort of child murderer embeds her victim's teeth in chocolate? The others start edging towards the door but you're driven now to solve this mystery and you can feel the answers are within your grasp.

'Aaaah ... Amelia, I totally understand what you did. I mean, it can happen to anyone, right? Mean Matron stealing chocolate, whipping children to death. Of course you wanted to avenge your friends. But why did you put her teeth in chocolate? Is it like ... some sort of ironic punishment?'

'Oh as if!' Amelia sounds scornful. 'I never got the chance to kill anyone. You should take a look at the book on the fourth shelf, third row down. *How to Best Little Beasties*. That's the book the Matron was reading to us at bedtime before she disappeared. It might have more clues.'

You're pretty sure Amelia's got another trick up her sleeve. Do not open that book (Turn to page 32)

You're on to Amelia now. Two steps forward, one step back. Opening the book will probably end badly but there might be a pretty valuable clue hidden within (Turn to page 59)

23

You can't see the harm in letting a disembodied voice out of the wall. Jessica shakes her head vehemently.

'Somebody put her in there for a reason,' she hisses.

You roll your eyes. 'Don't be paranoid. It might be a game of hide-and-seek gone wrong. Besides, she's probably got some good clues to finding the murderer.'

'I can take her if she tries anything funny,' Frankie growls, rolling his shoulders back and jabbing the air like a professional boxer. You climb up the ladder and release the latch.

Creeeeeeeeeaaaaaaaaakkkkkkkkk.

You jump back a safe distance, enough to give you a reasonable head start if she starts chasing. For a moment, there's nothing but dust motes.

Click. Click. Click. Cautiously, one bony foot dangles out of the door. It feels around daintily like a swimmer testing the water. Finding it safe, she places it on the first rung of the ladder. Crack.

A second bony foot appears. Crack. It's all you can do to stop from screaming. Amelia is a rotting skeleton. It wouldn't be so bad if she had been picked clean, like the smooth, shiny surfaces of Sam, the dancing skeleton the science teacher occasionally wheels into class. Amelia is still decomposing. There are fleshy chunks attached to her rib cage and a sunken eye sits in one socket. When she grins, you can see teeth wobbling through her partially rotten cheek.

Even though it's rude to stare, you can't look away.

'If we knew there were visitors, we would have put on our good dress.' Amelia brushes down the remains of a white pinafore.

'We?' Your eyes turn back towards the door. 'Who else is in there?'

She drops her head a little and then raises her eyes coyly. The back of your arms erupt in goose bumps.

'How do you know who the murderer is?' Angus demands. You feel a flash of annoyance. You're the leader. You should be doing the interrogating.

'The walls have ears,' Amelia drawls. 'First lets play a game of I Spy. I'll go first. I spy with my little eye something starting with M.'

You get a funny feeling in the bottom of your stomach.

'Murder?' Jessica starts edging towards the staircase. Amelia giggles and twists the hem of her raggedy dress in her hands.

'Meal?' Angus cowers behind Jessica even though he's twice her size.

'Matron! M is for Matron!'

You notice a fetid stench wafting down the hallway.

To your left, the broom closet door bursts open. A mother of a mummy lurches towards you, blocking the staircase. It's hard to see where her tattered gown ends and the soiled bandages begin. The linen starts unravelling across her distended stomach. She's brandishing a sword. Not a gentlemen's rapier for sparring but a heavy-duty sword with a solid metal hilt and a serrated blade.

She roars her displeasure.

Amelia giggles, 'Matron's turned into a Mummy.' She scurries back up the ladder to her door. 'Come quick and hide! There's no room for any more skeletons in the closet but there's plenty of space in the walls.'

THE END
(Return to page 13)

24

You hesitate for a moment and Frankie senses your weakness. He pushes you forward and runs full pelt for the door. The Doctor cackles.

'I don't need a check-up.' You back towards the wall. 'I brush my teeth morning and night.'

'A mouth full of rotten teeth makes you tell lies.'

There could be some truth in that. You have told a few big ones in the past. Maybe it's the lack of flossing.

Floss! That's it. If you could get your hands on some, you could strangle the Doctor. Or set up some sort of booby trap to trip him. Or … the Doc's hands snake out and grab you around the middle.

'Looking for this?' He's got a piano wire in one hand. 'Ordinary floss is no good. We need the strong stuff. This will clean out all those rotten candy shards caught between your teeth. Open wide!'

In the back of your mind, something clicks. What Amelia had heard were not the screams of whipped children. You clamp your mouth shut and shake your head from side to side.

'Let me out,' Amelia hisses but it's too late. A gas mask is slipped over your face. Your nostrils fill with warm air and something else. Something cold that hits the back of your throat and trickles into your lungs. Your eyes feel heavy.

'Count backwards from ten,' the Doc whispers.

Ten ... nine ... eight ... seven ... six ... five ... four ...

THE END
(**Return to page 37**)

25

'The fairy godmother,' Jessica breathes staring at the picture from *How to Best Little Beasties.*

'A fairy godmother on steroids,' Frankie corrects.

'A Bone Collector!' Angus reads the description underneath the picture. As soon as he says it, you hear a taunting chant, a voice crooning its way up the stairs.

'The spine bones connected to the face bones.
The face bones connected to the jaw bones.
The jaw bones connected to the tooth bones.
Oh see how they grow. Bones, bones, bones!'

You cast your eyes around frantically but it's too late. You have a knack of positioning yourself in a dead-end room. His voice bounces down the hallway.

'Dem bones, dem bones, dem knobbly bones.
Dem bones, dem bones, dem hobbly bones.
Dem bones, dem bones, dem wobbly bones.
Oh! See how they grow.'

He's scarier in person. The book doesn't quite convey the way he licks his cracked lips at the sight of four kids. Or the way he dances a little jig causing his knucklebone necklace to knock and rattle like a primitive instrument. Or the way he smells like an animal carcass dipped in acetone.

'Whaddiwee whaddiwee have heeeya?' he croons. He frowns slightly at the empty dental trolley. 'Whaddave you kids done with my dentist?' When no one answers, he leans forward, his nostrils flaring like a sniffer dog at an airport. 'Where are my bones?'

Frankie screams and does a runner. It's a stupid thing to do because the Bone Collector is blocking the doorway. His skeletal hand reaches out grabbing Frankie by the forearm.

'You have a well formed humerus,' he remarks in a conversational tone.

'Do something,' Jessica moans. One moment you don't know what to do. The next you seize *How to Best Little Beasties*. Your hands run down the page. The Bone Collector. Strengths: death like grip from skeletal hands, can tear bones off muscle, terrible sense of humour. Weakness: melts in acid.

You remember the garden shed on the way up to the house. What better place to store acidic chemicals? But first you need to get around the Bone Collector. You grab a chair, determined to batter your way through. The Bone Collector senses your attack and turns. You veer left. Suddenly your foot gives way. It's one of the Coke bottles Frankie brought up after the chocolate binge. The bottle flies through the air. As the bubbles build inside, the loose cap flies off spraying sugar free soft drink in the Bone Collector's face.

'Aaaarrggggghhhh!' He drops Frankie to claw at his face. Frankie staggers backward and falls over another bottle. You meet his eyes for one second. As if connected by telepathy, everyone scrambles for the remaining bottles.

'Shake it up!' You order but there's no need to give instructions. Frankie's uncapped his bottle hitting the Bone Collector in the face. Jessica's gleefully shooting spurts of Coke at his torso. Angus struggles with the cap for a second and releases a puddle at the Bone Collector's feet.

There's a slightly burnt smell as the Bone Collector starts to melt. His clothes are singed and there's a sickening sizzling sound like slapping raw meat on a BBQ.

'This is for all the kids of Goultown!' Jessica cheers as his legs snap from under him.

'This is for Amelia!' You chime in. There's an appreciative tap-tap on the far side of the wall.

'This is for putting your hand under my pillow at night!' Frankie yells.

'And for only paying two dollars per tooth, you tight-ass!' Angus adds.

Nothing is left but a soaked rag and a knucklebone necklace. Jessica stoops down and examines the trinket.

'It's made from my teeth,' Amelia pipes up through the wall. 'Could I have it back please?'

It seems a fitting end after the help she's provided. You try sliding the necklace under the crack in the secret door but the molar catches. What are you going to do? Amelia seems to sense your predicament.

'You could open the door. After all our adventures together, I think I've proven I'm quite trustworthy,' she purrs.

Aargggh. More decisions. You scoop up the necklace and put it in your pocket. Thankfully, this is one decision that will be deferred for another time.

THE END (for real)

CHOOSE YOUR OWN DEATH

MARIANNA SHEK

Dearest Reader

I hope my creepy story has brought you a little joy. This project started as a small commission for a magazine, but when the project kept growing, I decided to find my own way of getting the story out to the readers.

I had a lot of support to make this happen.

Firstly, a sincere thank you to Tara Brown my illustrator who jumped on board before she'd even finished reading my first draft.

Thank you to my editor Nicole Ingram and my beta readers Annie Shek, Johanna Barclay, Gert Geyer, Peter Moyes. Thank you also for the advice, knowledge and technical support – Debbie Terranova, Emily Craven, James Warr and Gordon Moyes.

Finally, the path of writers and illustrators is tough, frustrating and often squeezed into the in-between spaces (I am currently writing this during my day job!) If you like this story, please help out by sharing with your family and friends at www.rockonkitty.com.au

Until the next story,
Marianna

CHOOSE YOUR OWN DEATH